TOLLINS 2:

DYNAMITE TALES

First published in hardback in Great Britain by HarperCollins Children's Books 2011

HarperCollins Children's Books is a division of HarperCollins Publishers Ltd
77-85 Fulham Palace Road, Hammersmith, London W6 8JB

Visit us on the web at www.harpercollins.co.uk

1

Text © Conn Iggulden 2011
Illustrations © Lizzy Duncan 2011

ISBN 978-0-00-730401-1

Conn Iggulden and Lizzy Duncan reserve the right to be identified as the author and illustrator of the work.

Printed and bound in China

CONN IGGULDEN

TOLLINS2:
DYNAMITE TALES

Illustrated by
LIZZY DUNCAN

Harper Tollins *Children's Books*

FOR SOPHIE
AND ARTHUR

CONN
IGGULDEN

FOR ROB,
MUM AND DAD

LIZZY
DUNCAN

CONTENTS

BLUE THUNDER

WANGLE

DAWLISH

THE HIGH DARK TOLLIN
(MAGNUS)

THE HIGH TOLLIN
(ALBERT)

CAST OF CHARACTERS

YELLOW PERIL

GRUNION   SPARKLER   WING   BERYL   PILFORD

OXFORD

CHORLEYWOOD

SOUTHEND-ON-SEA

HENLEY-ON-THAMES

LONDON

WINCHESTER

BRIGHTON

ISLE OF
WIGHT

C H A N N E L –

BOOK ONE

ROMEO AND BERYL

[A TALE OF TWO TOLLINS]

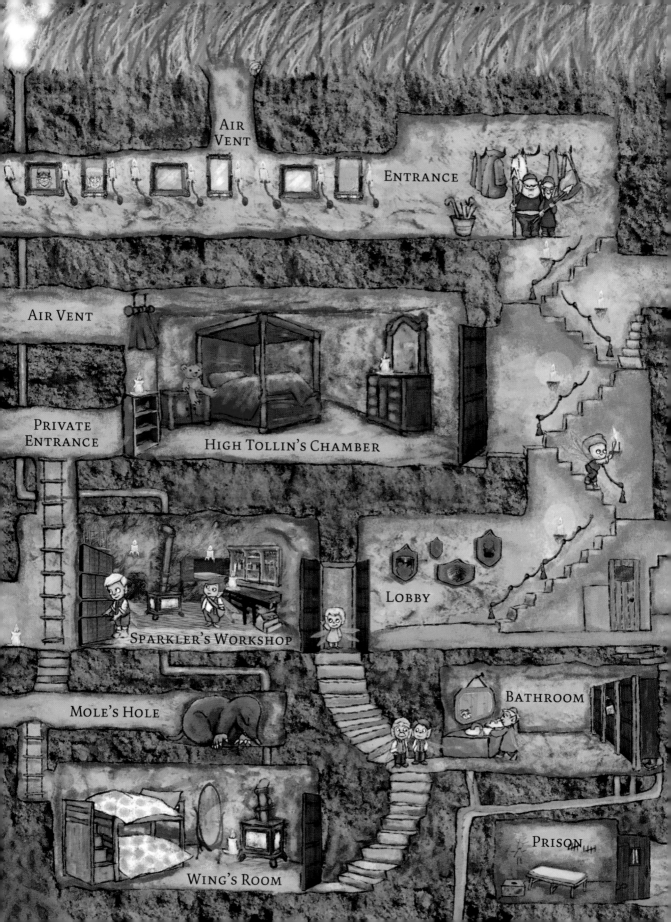

AIR VENT

ENTRANCE

AIR VENT

PRIVATE
ENTRANCE

HIGH TOLLIN'S CHAMBER

SPARKLER'S WORKSHOP

LOBBY

MOLE'S HOLE

BATHROOM

WING'S ROOM

PRISON

CHAPTER ONE

THE YEAR 1924, DURING THE REIGN OF KING GEORGE V

 PARKLER COULDN'T HELP HIMSELF. The sun was a ball of pleasant gold, the clouds looked a bit like sheep with no legs and he was happy. The only cloud on his horizon, except of course for the ones that actually *were* on the horizon, (sheep, no legs) was his secret. A secret that made you happy was a difficult one to keep. He knew he had to tread carefully. Not everyone picked up after their dogs, you see.

This particular secret involved books and not the ones he had so carefully copied out before, either. A new thing had come to Chorleywood that summer. Tollins do not often take much notice of human affairs and Sparkler could have missed it if he hadn't been out training a dragonfly to hunt beetles.

It had seemed like a good idea at the time. A dragonfly is a bit like a hawk on a smaller scale – a Tollin scale. They are fast and agile and they can catch almost anything in the air. Sparkler's dragonfly would sit on his sleeve if he fed it titbits, but he was beginning to think that its four wings and glittering body were a sort of beautiful covering for what was, in the end, a very dim insect indeed. The one he was training seemed more interested in nipping his ears than bringing savage destruction to edible prey.

It had been Sparkler's idea to train the insects, but somehow, he just didn't seem to have the knack for it. Half the dragonflies on Darvell's Pond had been retrained for hunting, racing or even formation flying, while his just sulked and turned its back on him. He regretted naming it now, obviously. Grunion's one was known as 'Blue Thunder' and brought its master all sorts of delicious things for the oven. Wing had one she called 'Lightning' and even her father had managed to train one he called the 'Yellow Peril'.

Sparkler shook his head as he looked at young Wolfenstein. It wasn't a great name, even with the hint of wolf in it. It certainly wasn't a great name for a dragonfly that seemed to prefer being fed by hand and sleeping to any hunting at all.

He had come across his secret one bright morning, as he had been trying to get Wolfenstein to respond to whistle signals. Sparkler had seen a heavy lorry arrive in a cloud of dust and he ducked down in the long grass to watch. Wolfenstein stuck his head up in the air and Sparkler had to sit on him to keep him still.

The lorry had stopped at the new Memorial Hall, its brakes squealing. Sparkler watched in fascination as a man smoking a pipe began to unload wooden boxes. It was too interesting to resist and Sparkler waited until the man went inside before nipping across and peering into a box. Books!

Human books wrapped in twine! He had never seen so many before. In fact, he hadn't known there were so many books in the world.

He and Wolfie were back across the road in the long grass before the man returned to finish unloading. There were now old ladies in the hall. Sparkler could see them through the window. He couldn't see their legs, which gave them the look of ships drifting back and forth. He wondered if they had been in the boxes, with the books. In all honesty, that didn't seem likely, but he was too excited to think straight.

Sparkler had avoided human books almost completely since the time he'd cured the High Tollin's gout, but they still called to him. He'd seen them lurking on shelves in human houses, sometimes covered in dust and unloved. He'd wanted to take them home and show them affection and respect until their covers were bright and glossy again.

Now he knew where the humans kept their secret store.

All right, not very secret. The man with the pipe and boxes was hardly creeping about and it was broad daylight, but a room full of books? That was something new. Sparkler knew he had to tell someone. A secret that good can give you indigestion.

CHAPTER TWO

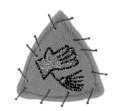

TEAM GRUNION

 PARKLER FOUND THE DRAGONFLY RACERS SLIGHTLY ANNOYING. Grunion had certainly changed. It wasn't just that he wore badges, or even the pride he took in the little cup he'd won for Pond Endurance. It wasn't even the plasters he wore on his ears, or getting up at dawn to train. He had found a hobby and Sparkler was pleased for him. He just wished he wouldn't take it all so seriously.

"I can't come on a raid with you," Grunion said, leafing through a manual with pictures of racing harnesses. "I need to be here for Blue Thunder's midnight feed, or he'll be sluggish in the morning. If we're going to beat that team of Red Needlers, he needs all the rest he can get."

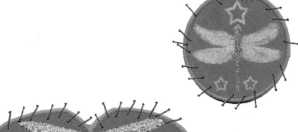

"Is it a 'he', Grunion?" Sparkler asked innocently. "How can you tell?"

"The markings," Grunion replied, without looking up. "It's the pattern of colour, you see, and the wings, which are..." His voice faded away as he became aware of Sparkler's stare. "All right, I don't know. I still can't come on a raid with you. Human books are forbidden anyway. I'm not getting into that kind of trouble again!"

Sparkler sighed to himself. He liked Grunion. The Tollin was kind and cheerful, but truth be told, he was a little bit timid. Not frightened, or cowardly, just not a fan of loud noises, surprises, or creeping about at night.

"All right, Grun," he said. "Good luck with the race tomorrow."

"We don't need luck," Grunion replied.

"We?" said Sparkler. "Are you racing as well then?"

"It's an expression. *We* are the team, Sparkler. Blue

Thunder and Grunion." Grunion leaned closer. "You know, I think they have a damselfly in that pack of reds. That's cheating, Sparkler! A damselfly!"

"Goodness," Sparkler said. "How, um, unsporting of them."

"Exactly!" Grunion replied. "Still, Blue Thunder is in fine form. I've only just finished waxing him."

"Him?"

"Or her. It's the pattern, or something. Or the wings."

Sparkler left his friend reading the instructions on a tin of wax with the High Tollin's face on it. That was another strange thing. Just days after Sparkler had mentioned the idea in conversation, there seemed to be products all the racers had to have, from special racing harnesses, to ear protectors and body wax.

Sparkler had even seen a poster for a thing he could have designed himself, which used a steel spring to launch targets into the air for training.

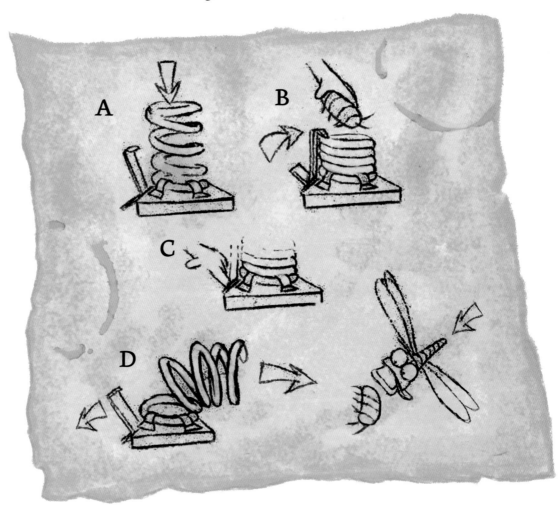

The world was changing. Ever since he'd lit the first tiny forge and produced a misshapen lump of black iron, everything was different. It was as if he'd unlocked something in his people and they didn't need him as much. He supposed he should be pleased about that, but somehow, he just wasn't.

He could have gone to Wing, or even old Briar. They would have understood the excitement he felt about a whole room of human books. Being turned down by Grunion had taken the fun out of it, somehow. Sparkler walked back across the common with his hands in his pockets, kicking idly at pebbles.

That night, Sparkler went alone to the Memorial Hall and squeezed through a gap under the roof-tiles. It was the largest building he had ever seen and every scratching sound he made echoed back at him as if there were someone else in there.

In the gloom, he flew down to the floor and fiddled with a piece of flint and iron that produced sparks. It wasn't easy, as each spark left green lines across his vision, but he managed to light a small lamp. Iron was amazing stuff, he'd discovered. He was working on a needle compass, but the one he had made just pointed north. That was fine if he wanted to go north, but he didn't always want to go that way.

The lamp lit up a row of shelves and he looked up, then up again. There they were. Row upon row of books, stretching away into the distance. When he'd found books before, it had always been in a house, where he could be disturbed at any moment. Here, there was no one. He read the human sign above the door. 'Library' sounded a little bit like liberty and it was freedom of a sort. All human knowledge was there and it was his. In a sort of joyous trance, he walked to a low shelf and

looked at his first title.

"*The Complete Works of Shakespeare,*" he read aloud. Shaking spears sounded pretty exciting and he liked to see how things worked. It was perfect. He heaved the book out on to the wooden floorboards and opened it, placing the lamp where the light could spill across the page. He would read this one first and then work his way down the shelf.

As dawn came to Chorleywood and the racing dragonflies were finishing their power breakfasts and being rubbed down, Sparkler was still there with that first book, his mouth hanging slightly open in amazement.

CHAPTER THREE

YOU CAN'T GO WRONG WITH A SWORDFIGHT

VER THE NEXT WEEK, Grunion's Blue Thunder won the half-mile endurance, and the three-legged race was abandoned after furious arguments. There wasn't another Race Day scheduled for a fortnight and some things returned to normal.

Laden with play scripts, Sparkler walked along the tunnels under Chorleywood station, heading for the Great Hall and the High Tollin, Albert. He hadn't wasted the week. He was absolutely certain that he couldn't admit to discovering plays from a human book. He had chosen one he thought would appeal to the High Tollin and copied the play on to a sheaf of his best paper. His packages rustled as he strode through the lamp-lit tunnels, like whispers in his mind. He glanced at the title as he went: *Romeo and Juliet*. Better than *Macbeth* anyway, which involved murdering a king. He was fairly sure the High Tollin would not approve of that. *Romeo and Juliet* also had murders, but this Shakespeare lad had put in a few comedy scenes as well. It had everything, in fact.

The High Tollin was busy with his advisors. Sparkler was disappointed to see that they seemed to be designing a new poster for the races. The High Tollin's daughter Wing was there and even she was engrossed in the conversation, talking about the possibility of using young Tillets as riders.

Sparkler cleared his throat. When that didn't work, he said "A-hem!" a little too loudly. The High Tollin put down the poster and beamed at him.

30

"Sparkler! Did you see my Yellow Peril this morning?"

"No, sir, but I'm sure it will clear up with a bit of cream," Sparkler replied, shuffling his papers. The High Tollin blinked at him.

"Yes… Now Sparkler, have you solved the problem of getting them to navigate long distances?"

Sparkler remembered vaguely that he had been asked to work on something for the dragonfly teams.

"Only if they want to go north," he muttered. "Or south, possibly. East or west would be…" He paused for a moment, thinking it through and picturing a compass in his mind.

"Oh," he said, smiling. "Yes, I have, your lordship. But that is not why I'm here."

Before the High Tollin could reply, Sparkler stepped up to the throne and handed over four packets of paper,

31

keeping one for himself. Wing took one and began to read it. The High Tollin looked confused, but he too opened the first page, while two of the advisors struggled to see over each other's shoulders.

"There are plenty to go around," Sparkler said. He'd had a whole class of Tillets copying out his first draft. He wasn't certain they'd managed the spelling of the trickier words, but the reaction had been good, at least.

"What is this?" the High Tollin said, in the tone of a man who'd expected more diagrams.

"It is... a play," Sparkler said. "You read the words aloud, as if it's real life."

He was dreading the next question. He'd thought of lots of ways to answer it, but if the word 'human' was part of it, he knew it would be the last he ever heard of plays. The book had set his imagination on fire. He couldn't let the High Tollin stamp out the flames, he just couldn't.

"Did you write it?" the High Tollin asked, unaware of how the words sent a shiver through Sparkler.

"Yes," Sparkler said in a tight whisper. It was true in a way. He had written each word. He just hadn't made them up. He just hoped William Shakespeare never heard about it.

"I'm not sure I quite understand," the High Tollin said, peering at the pages warily. "You read the words aloud, do you?"

"Yes, my lord. You learn them first and then you speak them as if it's all new. Other Tollins listen." Sparkler saw the High Tollin's eyes glaze over and struggled on.

"There are swordfights, my lord."

"Brilliant!" said the High Tollin immediately, as Sparkler had known he would. All the Tollins were fascinated by the new swords coming out of the iron forges. Grunion used one of the prototypes to cut his toenails.

"If you look... here, my lord," Sparkler went on, "you'll see a speech by an angry prince, a man of power and authority a little like yourself. He is angry with his people for fighting in the street... with swords."

"Brilliant!" said one of the advisors. The High Tollin frowned at him, then looked at the section Sparkler had indicated.

"Rebellious subjects, enemies to peace..." he read. "Oh, I like that. That's good, I shall use that."

"It's also a love story, my lord, a love story with swordfights."

"And the prince wins in the end, I expect? Executes his enemies and so on?"

"Well, yes, he does, in a way," Sparkler said reluctantly. He wasn't sure the High Tollin had understood the idea, but he hadn't refused it outright, either.

"That's good, lad. Well, thank you for bringing this to me. I shall put it with that book of herbs you made."

"Yes, well done," said one of the advisors. Sparkler glared at him until the advisor blushed and pretended to read the script.

"I would like to *perform* the play, my lord," Sparkler went on. "The Tillets are available for some of the smaller parts. I thought I might play Mercutio myself, Romeo's friend. He dies in a swordfight."

"Brilliant!" the same advisor murmured.

"Well... we are a little busy at the moment," said the High Tollin. "Does the prince have much to say? I mean, would it take me long to learn the words?"

Sparkler blinked. This was not how he had expected the conversation to run, or even limp.

"I could have just your character's lines copied out on to new paper, my lord. You could learn them in a month, I'm certain. I thought I might aim to perform the play at the end of summer, just before the leaves turn." He saw the High Tollin was engrossed in the lines.

"Once more, on pain of death, all men depart!" bellowed the High Tollin. His advisors were halfway out of the room before he called them back. "Oh, that was a great bit. I'm *definitely* using that one again."

"You might consider *not* shouting, my

36

lord," Sparkler said desperately.

"Oh, you need a bit of shouting," the High Tollin told him. "It makes people sit up and listen, shouting."

"I'll have to hold auditions, my lord," Sparkler added.

"Auditions?" said one of the advisors. Sparkler glared at him again.

"Yes, my lord. Anyone who wants to be in the play can read a few lines and then I choose the best ones."

"I see," the High Tollin said. A dangerous tone entered his voice. "I don't suppose there will be anyone else wanting to be the prince, though?"

"I seriously doubt it, my lord," Sparkler said, with a sigh.

"Excellent," said the High Tollin. "Shouting and executions. I am more than qualified, after all."

Sparkler gave in. Wing looked up from the play and grinned at him.

"Yes, my lord," he said.

CHAPTER FOUR

YOU CAN'T DO IT WITHOUT A BALCONY

ROTHE BY ANY OTHER NAME WOULD THMELL AS THWEEET!"

"Yes... yes, thank you, Beryl," Sparkler said. "I think I see the problem there."

The little Tillet looked downcast.

"Ith it my brathe, thir?"

"I'm sorry?"

"My brathe, thir, on my teeth!"

Sparkler didn't want to hurt Beryl's feelings. She'd always had a lisp, but he had to admit that the brace he'd designed for her front teeth seemed to make it worse. She had worked ever so hard copying out the scripts and it felt mean to refuse her a part.

"The thing is, Beryl, there are only four female parts in the play. Lady Montague is a mature lady, as is Lady Capulet. The nurse is meant to be quite old, so that leaves…"

"Juliet, thir, yeth, who ith quite young, like mythelf," said Beryl firmly. She did not intend to be denied her part by a few lines of train track running round her teeth. Even Sparkler wilted against that diamond stare.

"Right, Juliet then," he said at last. "Let's see how you get on during the rehearsals."

"Thank you, thir. You won't regret it," she said, beaming at him.

"Next!" Sparkler called. He watched impatiently as the High Tollin's guards shuffled up. Sparkler repressed a groan. This was getting out of hand. It was true he'd been given the Great Hall to stage the performance, but in return, the High Tollin seemed to want everyone he knew personally to be in it. Sparkler resolved to be firm.

"Right. Which part would you like to audition for?"
he asked.

"What's in a name?" the thin guard bellowed suddenly.
"That which we call a rose by any other name would smell as
sweet!"

"That's a line by Juliet," Sparkler said, searching his script.
He had never seen the guards so nervous before. The thin one
had taken a position with his eyes screwed shut, his arms
outstretched and his red face tilted up to an imaginary audience.

"It is the east! And Juliet
is the sun!" he roared.

"That bit's from Romeo,
I think," Sparkler said, wincing.
The guard seemed to be lost
in a world of his own.
His companion
looked on with tears

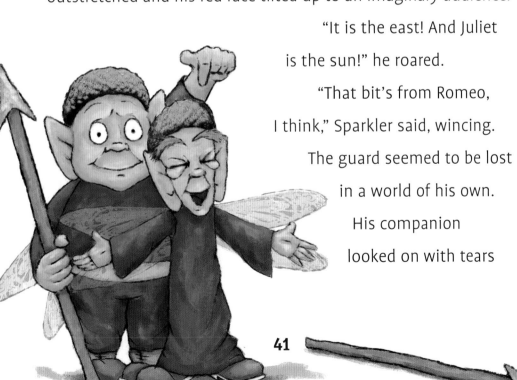

41

in his eyes, shaking his head in silent wonder.

"Arise, fair sun!" the thin guard shouted, drawing his new sword. Sparkler gaped as he waved it around his head. "And *kill* the envious moon!"

"Some confusion there, I'm afraid," Sparkler said in the pause for breath. The guard opened his mouth for another line.

"Thank you! I've heard enough!" Sparkler said loudly. His tone seemed to reach the guard and he opened his eyes, beaming shyly.

"Was it all right, sah? I've been practising with Daryl here. He says I've got ever such good volume."

"Well, yes," Sparkler replied. "I can't argue with *volume*. Volume, in fact, is the one thing no one could deny about your performance. However..."

"I wouldn't mind a small part, sah," the fat guard put in suddenly. Sparkler supposed this was Daryl, though he'd never heard his name before. He sighed to himself. It was the High

Tollin's Great Hall, after all. It was the only place he could find with a balcony.

"All right," he said wearily. "You can both be in Romeo's gang of Montagues and in the crowd scenes." Daryl nodded to his thinner friend.

"I told you we'd get it, 'Erbert," he said proudly.

"Next!" Sparkler called once again.

Finding Romeo was the real problem, of course. In the play, he was meant to be young and handsome. There *were* young and handsome Tollins, but the news that Beryl was to play Juliet had made them vanish faster than frost in summer.

To his frustration, Sparkler was left with just one Tollin lad, by the name of Pilford, who worked in the bakery. He was short and thin and his hair was too long, in Sparkler's opinion.

"So you want to be Romeo, do you?" Sparkler said doubtfully.

"Don't mind," Pilford replied with a shrug. Sparkler peered behind him, but there was no one. Pilford *was* the queue.

"Have you prepared any lines for today?" Sparkler asked. Pilford nodded. "Right then. In your own time, let's hear them."

Pilford looked around him. The High Tollin's guards were nearby, listening while pretending to read a script. Some Tillets were watching him, including one with enormous front teeth. He shrugged again.

"Right. It's the bit at the end where everyone gets killed. My mum cried when I did it."

"When you're ready," Sparkler said.

"Romeo thinks Juliet is dead, though she isn't," Pilford went on.

"Yes, I've read the scene," Sparkler replied. "Wrote it, I

mean. Er... in your own time."

"And he kills 'imself and then *she wakes up*! My mum was blubbering fit to burst when she 'eard me do that bit."

"Are we going to experience this treat today, do you think?" Sparkler asked.

"So Juliet finds her love all dead and curled up and that, so she stabs 'erself! It was brilliant, that bit. I'd have put a swordfight in the background, just for added interest, you know, but it was pretty good anyway. My mum enjoyed all the 'thees' and 'thys' instead of just saying 'you' and 'yours' – she said it made it proper old-fashioned-sounding and ever so romantic. I think you have a fan there, sir."

Sparkler opened his mouth to send him away, but Pilford threw out an arm and began. His voice became larger somehow, so that it filled the space.

"O, my love, my wife! Death that hath sucked the honey of thy breath, Hath had no power yet upon thy beauty. Thou art not conquered; beauty's ensign yet is crimson in thy lips and in thy cheeks, And death's pale flag is not advanced there..."

There was silence in the Great Hall. The guards stood with their mouths open, though that was not unusual when they were off-duty. Beryl's eyes glittered with tears.

"I think we have a Romeo," Sparkler said softly. Pilford's shoulders slumped.

"Sorry to hear that, sir. I was looking forward to having a go at him."

"No, Pilford. I mean you're it. That was... good."

"Really, sir?" Pilford beamed at him. "Mum will be ever so pleased."

47

CHAPTER FIVE

MAGIC AND FALSE TEETH

HAT SUMMER WAS ONE OF THE HOTTEST IN TOLLIN MEMORY and the Common basked in the warm days. Small human children ran about with big dogs, while some big children ran about with small dogs. The long grass was a tapestry of butterflies, with colours of red and gold and sometimes a bit of yellow, even. Dragonflies buzzed on Darvell's Pond, chasing their own bright reflections on the water while Tollins on the bank shouted things like, "More angle on the turns, Flaming Death! You have four wings, so use them! Flaming *Nuisance*, more like!"

In the halls under Chorleywood Station, the play had taken over. There was no other description for it. Perhaps it was

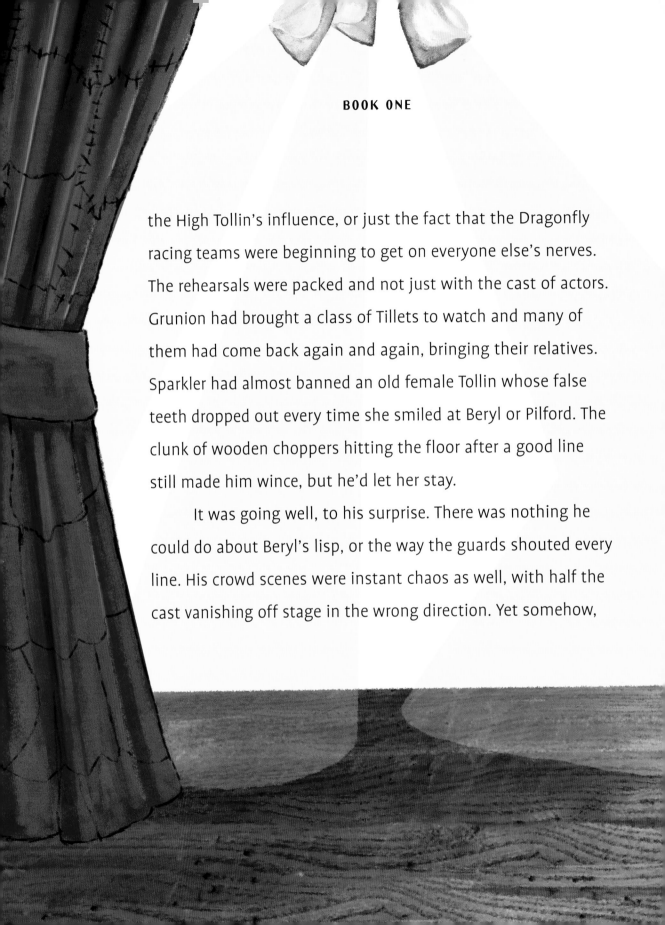

the High Tollin's influence, or just the fact that the Dragonfly racing teams were beginning to get on everyone else's nerves. The rehearsals were packed and not just with the cast of actors. Grunion had brought a class of Tillets to watch and many of them had come back again and again, bringing their relatives. Sparkler had almost banned an old female Tollin whose false teeth dropped out every time she smiled at Beryl or Pilford. The clunk of wooden choppers hitting the floor after a good line still made him wince, but he'd let her stay.

It was going well, to his surprise. There was nothing he could do about Beryl's lisp, or the way the guards shouted every line. His crowd scenes were instant chaos as well, with half the cast vanishing off stage in the wrong direction. Yet somehow,

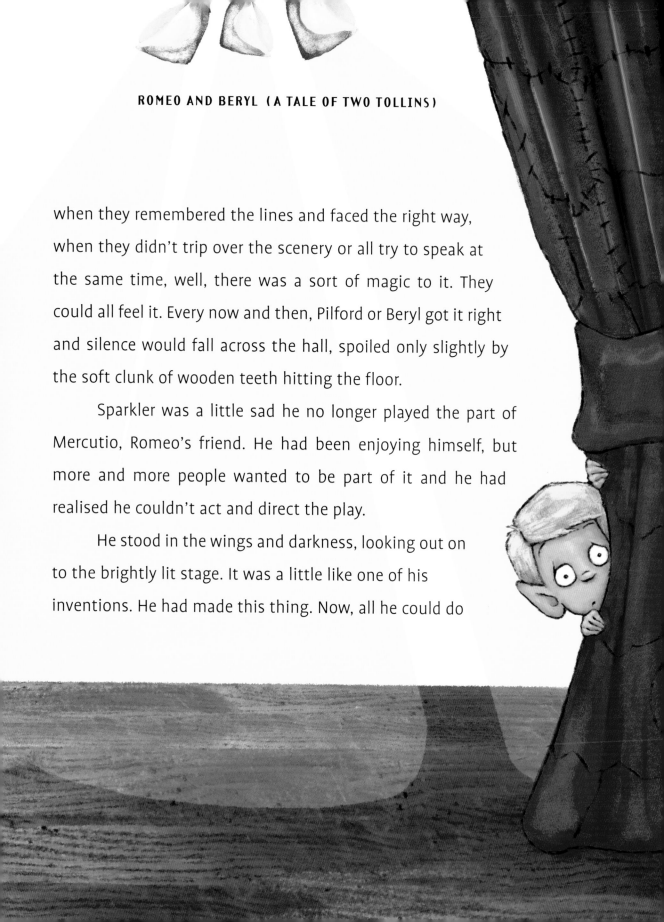

ROMEO AND BERYL (A TALE OF TWO TOLLINS)

when they remembered the lines and faced the right way, when they didn't trip over the scenery or all try to speak at the same time, well, there was a sort of magic to it. They could all feel it. Every now and then, Pilford or Beryl got it right and silence would fall across the hall, spoiled only slightly by the soft clunk of wooden teeth hitting the floor.

Sparkler was a little sad he no longer played the part of Mercutio, Romeo's friend. He had been enjoying himself, but more and more people wanted to be part of it and he had realised he couldn't act and direct the play.

He stood in the wings and darkness, looking out on to the brightly lit stage. It was a little like one of his inventions. He had made this thing. Now, all he could do was stand back and hope it worked when it had to. Tollins were not cogs and springs, of course, or even mouse intestines and a steam chamber. There were still mistakes, almost every day, but the actors were becoming more confident. He'd even seen Pilford wipe a tear from his eye after a good rehearsal, though it might have been spit from standing too close to Beryl's lisp.

Sparkler noticed silence had come to the stage and he waited for the clunk that would reveal a good line. It didn't come.

"Are you all right, Pilford?" Sparkler hissed. He checked his script. "'Courage man, the hurt cannot be much...' Pilford? '*Courage* man, the hurt...'"

Pilford stood, swaying slightly. When Sparkler realised he wasn't going to continue, he walked out of the wings and on to the stage, past the black curtains specially made by the Tollin Ladies' Association. As he reached Pilford, he saw Beryl's face was showing horror and he halted.

"Pilford?" he said.

"I'm sorry, sir. I don't feel very…" Pilford vomited on the stage and Sparkler leaped backwards rather than be splashed. He heard a clunk behind him and turned to the seats in irritation.

"That's not part of the play, madam," he said irritably. "He's really ill!"

Sparkler felt Pilford's forehead and found it burning hot.

"Oh, this isn't good," he said.

"Sorry, sir," Pilford replied. "I've been feeling a bit wonky for a day or two now."

"Thir?" Beryl said, behind him.

"Not now, Beryl," Sparkler snapped. This was a disaster. The play posters had gone up all over the tunnels. If Pilford didn't get well again quickly, the whole thing was ruined.

"Thir?" Beryl said again. Sparkler whipped round.

"Beryl? This is not the time, understand? If Pilford is sick..." He realised Beryl was looking oddly pale and as

realisation dawned, she vomited on to his shoes.

In the silence that followed, the cast stood in shock, looking at each other. In the echoing Great Hall, a small clunk almost made Sparkler lose his temper completely.

"*Still* not part of the play, madam!" he shouted. "Now put them back in and keep them there!"

CHAPTER SIX

APPARENTLY, THE SHOW MUST GO ON

T WAS THE NIGHT OF THE PLAY, the end of summer, with the leaves turning gold on the common. Deep below the station, the Great Hall was filled to the rafters with Tollins. Small lamps lit the stage and the air was warm and smelled of oil and make-up, of sawdust and fear. Sparkler was more nervous than he could believe. He'd known he couldn't cancel the play, not with so many Tollins looking forward to it. Pilford and Beryl were tucked up in their beds with hot drinks, very sorry to be missing out. Three of his Montagues had come down with the bug as well, though sadly not the High Tollin's guards.

Sparkler had explained to the cast that the play must go on, regardless of disasters. That too, was part of the magic, or so he'd read. Somehow, no matter what happened, it would be all right on the night. He hoped. Probably anyway.

He stood on the stage, dressed in a costume copied faithfully from *The Complete Works of Shakespeare*. The Tollin Ladies' Association had been surprised by parts of the design. Sparkler wasn't at all sure why you had to dress like that to be in a play, but he could hardly ask Shakespeare. The tights were slightly baggier than the picture and he wasn't at all sure about the ruff round his neck. It was a little too big, which meant he couldn't see his feet.

He found himself perspiring as he looked up at the balcony and not just from the heat of the lamps. He saw Wing appear there, dressed in a gown of green. For a moment, he just stood there, gazing upwards. As Juliet, Wing wasn't supposed to know he was there beneath her

58

balcony, but as the silence grew, she looked down and raised her eyebrows at him. She was enjoying this much more than he was. There hadn't even been time to practise the kissing scene. He just hoped he wouldn't make a fool of himself.

The words came, suddenly flooding out of him as if someone had pulled a lever. The audience settled back, some of them nudging each other. He told her he would change his name if she didn't like it and she told him her relatives would kill him if they knew he'd climbed in through the orchard. They talked of love and Wing's eyes were shining by the end. Some of the Ladies' Association were dabbing their eyes as well.

In just a few short lines, he and Juliet had promised they would meet at a chapel and be married. By the time they were, Romeo's fate was in motion and his best friend would be killed in front of him.

Sparkler and Wing moved through

the play as if the other actors were ghosts. The magic had taken hold of them. The moment came when they were to kiss and Sparkler felt his heart thump almost painfully in his chest. Their lips touched.

"Arrest that Tollin!" roared a voice. The audience froze and Sparkler looked past Wing to where the High Tollin was furiously waving a sword at him. One of his advisors was clinging to his arm.

"Arrest him for kissing my daughter! What? What do you mean we've discussed this? I don't remember... oh, oh yes. Ah. Um, Sorry, sorry, everyone, do carry on..."

The crowd relaxed back into their seats and Romeo was banished from the city forever. One of the High Tollin's guards sobbed as he delivered the news.

When Romeo heard Juliet was dead and went to her tomb, the crowd was silent

60

with awe and fear. They knew she was not truly dead and when he took poison to be with her, they gasped in horror. Old Briar even rose from his seat and shouted in tears, "She lives, lad! She lives!" but it was too late. Sparkler sank down and then Wing woke at last from her long sleep, waiting for her love. She found her Romeo dead beside her and she drew a dagger and ended her own life. In the deathly silence, there was a faint clunk.

At the end, when the actors and actresses came out on the stage to show they were not in fact *really* dead, the audience applauded wildly. Sparkler and Wing stood together in the centre of the line and bowed deeply, smiling at them all.

"You'll have to do it again, you know, when Beryl and Pilford are better," Wing murmured. "She was really sad to have missed this."

"Don't worry," Sparkler said, thinking of *The Complete Works*. "I have a few other plays in mind." He bowed again as the audience didn't seem to want to stop clapping.

"I didn't write it, you know, the play," he said to Wing over the noise.

"Oh, I knew that," Wing replied. Sparkler turned to her in surprise.

"How?"

"It doesn't have any machines in it."

"Well, no, it wasn't perfect. There's always room for improvement."

THE END OF
BOOK ONE

BOOK TWO

RADIO

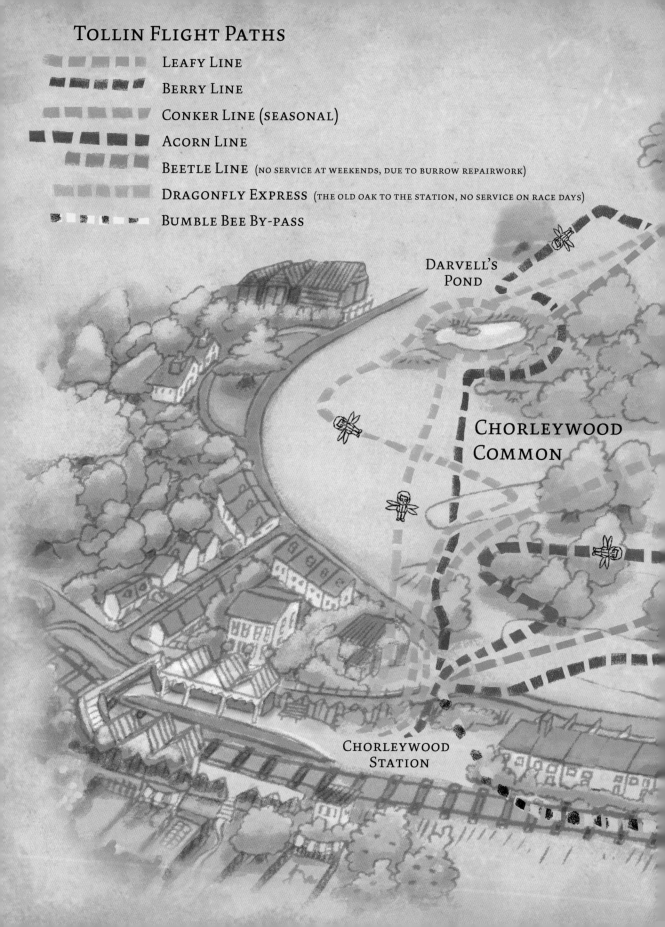

Tollin Flight Paths

- Leafy Line
- Berry Line
- Conker Line (seasonal)
- Acorn Line
- Beetle Line (no service at weekends, due to burrow repairwork)
- Dragonfly Express (the old oak to the station, no service on race days)
- Bumble Bee By-pass

Darvell's Pond

Chorleywood Common

Chorleywood Station

THE
OLD OAK

UP

LEFT   RIGHT

DOWN

CHAPTER ONE

THE AUTUMN OF 1924

T WAS A DARK AND BLUSTERY NIGHT. It was certainly not a night for flying. The rain was too heavy and the wind too dangerous for anything as small and light as a Tollin.

Yet Grunion and Sparkler were out in it. Not only that, they were trying to carry something larger than the pair of them put together. In a strange way, the heavy object acted as an anchor so they couldn't be blown away.

"What sort of night d'you call this?" Grunion said.* They were struggling to cross a road that had become a gleaming river down the centre of Chorleywood village.

"That is exactly my point, Grun!" said Sparkler, blowing and gasping. "If we can get this working, we could listen to the

* Dark and blustery.

weather forecast. We'd never be caught in a storm again!"

The wind had risen and Grunion had to shout to be heard.

"It still feels like stealing," he said. "That boy built it for the science fair in the Memorial Hall."

"Which was *yesterday*," Sparkler shouted back over the wind. "He'd clearly finished with it." He saw Grunion's doubtful

look and realised he had to say something more. Without warning, the wind dropped, leaving him talking too loud.

"Look, I can't make it myself," he went on. "I've read the books and there are bits I can't understand. I need to look at this one, take it apart maybe. After that, if you'll help me, I'll take it back to him, all right? That won't be stealing then. That will be *borrowing*."

"I think you have to ask, before you can call it borrowing," Grunion replied.

"All right, how about I go back tomorrow and leave something in exchange?" Sparkler shouted.

"Like what?"

"A firework? He'd enjoy playing with that."*

"Let's just get this thing home before someone sees us. With all this rain, it might not even work."

"It *will* work, Grun," Sparkler replied, his eyes bright with excitement. "I'll make it work."

★ ★ ★ ★ ★

73

* *Only once. After that, no fingers.*

The small hours of the morning always get a rough deal. They are actually the same size as other hours. They don't really mind 'small', but they seriously object to the 'wee, small hours', which just sounds insulting.

During those hours after midnight, a bedraggled, soaked figure buzzed wearily through the rain. Dawlish had flown all night and he was exhausted. He had lost track of the hours, large or indeed wee. He couldn't see the stars or the moon under all that cloud and he had lost his way. For a Tollin, it was a physical struggle to fly through the raindrops and wind. He was flung up and down, backwards then forwards. He was battered and bruised and weary, but he struggled on anyway.

A particularly vicious gust blew him into a wooden sign, making him dizzy for a while. He lay in the long grass and

looked up at it. He couldn't read human letters. If he had been able to, he'd have known it said 'Chorleywood'.

Wearily, he forced himself on. The rain died down before dawn and he found the train track and knew he was close. The station wasn't far and though he hadn't been there before, he was Tollin enough to find the tiny, hidden entrances that led to the tunnels deep below. He had made it and he was safe. He collapsed in a dry spot and went to sleep, just a few minutes before the High Tollin tripped over him and began yelling for his guards.

CHAPTER TWO

WHEN SLIPPERS ARE NOT THE RIGHT CHOICE

THE HIGH TOLLIN'S GUARDS had a firm grip on their prisoner as he was dragged into the Great Hall. The High Tollin was still flustered. He was not used to coming out of his bathroom and stumbling over a stranger. In fact, he was not used to strangers. The Tollins of Chorleywood all knew each other. Seeing a Tollin he did not know brought back terrible memories of the struggle with the Dark Tollins from Dorset. The High Tollin suspected his voice had gone a little high with the shock of it, so soon after brushing his teeth. He was covering his embarrassment with dignity and sheer indignation, though the effect was slightly spoiled by his bathrobe and slippers.

"Will the prisoner identify himself?" he demanded. Dawlish opened his mouth to reply and one of the guards cuffed him on the back of his head.

"Answer the High Tollin!" the guard bellowed. Dawlish could not rub his head, as his hands were bound in iron chains, which clanked nicely and were much more impressive than the old wooden ones. Instead, he glared at the guard.

"I'll remember you, mate," he said. The guard grinned evilly and then checked Dawlish's chains were secure, just in case.

"Name's Dawlish, sir," Dawlish said after a pause. "From Dorset."

"A *Dark* Tollin?" one of the advisors exclaimed in horror. The other advisors shuddered as they recalled the plot to overthrow their beloved High Tollin.

"I flew night and day, sir, to get to

78

Chorleywood. To warn you all, sir."

"He could be a spy, sir," one of the advisors murmured.

"A what?" the High Tollin replied.

"A spy, sir?"

"Ah! And a 'spy' is...?"

The advisor sighed.

"I'm sure we've been over this, sir. A spy is someone who creeps about and reports on us for our enemies, a *wicked* creature."

The High Tollin glared at Dawlish.

"Is he? I see," he said.

"I'm not a spy!" Dawlish snapped. "I've come here to warn you."

"He might not even be from Dorset, sir," said the advisor. "Quick, prisoner, how long did it take you to get here?"

Dawlish shrugged.

"Aboat a mumf," he said in his Dorset accent. Silence fell in the Great Hall.

"Some sort of code, was it?" the High Tollin whispered.

"I think he meant to say, 'About a month', sir."

"Oh, I see. He should try that old rhyme. How now... brown... what was that thing with horns?"

"Was it a Viking, sir?"

"Don't be silly, man. A cow, that was it. 'How now, brown cow?' It helps you speak properly, as I understand it."

Dawlish watched all this in fascination. He had been told the Chorleywood Tollins were intelligent and dangerous folk, with more ideas than they knew what to do with. He was beginning to believe he had been misled.

At that moment, two young Tollins entered the Great Hall in a rush.

"Sparkler! And my dear Wing," said the High Tollin. "Thank you for coming. Wing, would you mind fetching my work shoes?"

"In a minute, Father," Wing replied. "Who is the prisoner?"

"He is a Dark Tollin spy, apparently. We've been interrogating him."

Sparkler was watching Dawlish with some interest. He saw a young and grubby Tollin who was very close to losing his temper completely. Sparkler sympathised. He'd once been in the same position. Dawlish felt his steady gaze and turned his head until they were staring at each other.

"You told them you were a spy?" Sparkler said. Dawlish shook his head and sighed.

"No. I told them I'd come to warn you all." He waited, but with Sparkler present, no one else seemed to want to interrupt.

81

"Well?" Sparkler said. "What was the warning then?"

Dawlish considered. He'd come a long way to help these people and instead of being grateful, they'd chained him up, thrown him on the floor and accused him of being a wicked creature. He was almost ready to forget about helping them, but the new one did seem a little sharper than the wrinkled old one.

"You're about to be invaded," he said at last. "There's an army on the way."

"*What*?" the High Tollin demanded. "You didn't think to mention this before?"

"While your guards were chaining me up, perhaps?" Dawlish said. "Or dragging me through the tunnels to this place?"

"You could've walked," the fat guard mumbled. "You only had to say."

"I didn't want to go with you!" Dawlish snapped.

"Draggin's the only option then," the guard murmured,

staring at the floor.

"Get those chains off him," Sparkler said. The guards looked to the High Tollin and he nodded, struck dumb with terror. It was Wing who took the keys from his belt and unlocked the chains. Dawlish rubbed his wrists and glared around him. The thin guard, Herbert, tried to hide behind the fat one and was surprisingly successful.

"You will need to summon your war council, High Tollin," Dawlish said, taking a deep breath.

"War council?" the High Tollin said, his voice going squeaky again. He cleared his throat. "I don't have one of those. My advisors are all... um... here."

"Oh dear," Dawlish said. "In that case, I think you could be in serious trouble."

CHAPTER THREE

MAKING WAVE

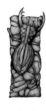N HIS WORKSHOP, Sparkler was testing the science fair project. Dawlish and Grunion were both watching him and for once, there was a grudging respect on the face of the Dorset Tollin.

"It picks up radio waves. They're in the air, you see. The amazing thing is that it doesn't even seem to need a power source."*

Sparkler's workshop was somewhere in the tunnels under the station. He'd insisted on blindfolding Dawlish before taking him there. He didn't bother blindfolding Grunion. Grunion always had to be led out anyway. He could get lost in his own living room. The workshop contained very little, except a long

* Surprisingly, for simple, home-made radios, this is true.

bench and racks of tools. Most of them were made of wood or shell, but there were one or two made of metal and Dawlish had been amazed to find a spool of wire. Admittedly, Sparkler had found it practically abandoned on a shop shelf, with a price tag, but that wasn't stealing, that was *finding* and it wasn't as if the humans ever missed that sort of thing.

The contraption on the bench looked strange, even by Sparkler's standards. It involved metal wire wound round and round a tube, with little loops sticking out. The most surprising bit was the telephone handset attached to it. That was the heavy part that had almost ruptured Grunion as he tried to carry it the night before.

As Sparkler moved little metal clips up and down the wire, a strange unearthly voice came out of the telephone. It was slower than Tollin speech and it rumbled on and on, like distant thunder.

86

"... and in Rockall, the wind is mainly east, five to seven; the sea is moderate to rough, with occasional rain... and that is the end of the shipping forecast..."

"Human voices!" Dawlish said, with a gasp. "That's incredible."

"It's just science," Sparkler muttered. "The radio waves are there all the time, going through us. All the receiver does—"

"Hang on," Grunion said suddenly. "Going *through* us? Right now, as I'm speaking, they're going through me?" He covered his stomach protectively.

"They don't do you any harm, Grun. At least, I can't see how they could," Sparkler replied absently. He was deep in thought. A radio could hear voices over a long distance, that much was obvious. What he needed was to be able to throw his own voice back. Before it had just been a project, an exciting new idea. With the threat from the south, though, it could play a vital part when the Dark Tollins arrived. If he could just get it to work. He was wary of taking the human boy's radio apart until he understood it, but he couldn't understand it without taking it apart. Life was like that sometimes.

He hadn't told Grunion about the torch he'd removed from the library cupboard in the Memorial Hall. It had a battery inside and he didn't want to explain the whole 'borrowing' thing again. He'd make it all right somehow, but he needed a battery if he was ever going to send his own voice back.

He propped his notebook up on the bench, vaguely aware of Dawlish staring at it in fascination. Sparkler didn't show him

the human book of *101 Things to Do* where he'd found the
original diagrams. He wasn't yet sure if he trusted Dawlish, not
completely anyway.

It was an odd thought. He wasn't used to distrusting any Tollin. Yet there was Dawlish, peering at his private notebook and making Sparkler uncomfortable.

"Why don't you go and show Dawlish the pond, Grunion?" Sparkler said, closing the book with a snap. "You could show him Blue Thunder, doing that turn thing."

Grunion looked coldly at his friend. It was a bone of contention between them that Sparkler didn't take dragonfly racing seriously enough.

"It's called a Wing Stall, Spark, as you very well know. He has mastered it, as it happens. Come on, Dawlish. You're going to love this."

Dawlish seemed reluctant, but Sparkler waved him off with his friend and then when he was alone, he really set to work. He needed more batteries for what he had in mind. If it came off, it would teach the Dark Tollins an important lesson.

CHAPTER FOUR

THE PROBLEM WITH HEDGEROWS

DORSET IS ABOUT NINETY MILES to the south and west of Chorleywood. It is an area on the south coast of England which is extremely pretty. The humans there enjoy the sea-breezes and frequently tell each other how bracing it all is. They make a point of doing things more slowly than Londoners, because, well, just because they can. Doing things slowly is sometimes a good thing. Building a house of cards is better if done slowly, while running for a bus should be quick. Eating a steak-and-kidney pie should definitely be slow, while drinking medicine should definitely be quick. Leading an army to war should also be quick, as any great general will tell you. You do not muck about during the frontal assault, stopping to buy postcards, then sucking your pen as you consider what to write home.

And so on. That is *not* the right way to launch a major offensive.

Wangle was one Dark Tollin who understood little rules like that. He was not a pleasant Dark Tollin. It was thanks to Tollins like Wangle that the Dorset clan were still called Dark Tollins by everyone else, instead of something more to do with the countryside, like Sheep-dip Tollins, say, or Wurzels. No one in London knows what a Wurzel is, but it does sound a bit *country* and quite nice.

Wangle had tried once before to take over the Chorleywood tunnels. That had been a sneak attack and ended with him being flooded out and washed away, when Sparkler had invented a pump. Wangle had learned a few lessons from that experience. He had learned to swim, for a start. More importantly, he had learned that not everything the humans did was wrong. If human books had been such a help to Chorleywood Tollins, he reasoned, perhaps they might be useful to Dark ones as well.

It is perhaps unfortunate that one of the first books he found was *The Ladybird Book of Battles*. He couldn't read it then, of course, though he'd enjoyed the pictures of explosions. It had taken him less than two years to learn to read, which isn't bad, start to finish. He learned so quickly because Wangle was driven. Not in the sense of being taken around in a car, obviously. 'Driven' in the sense of having a mission. His mission was simple. His mission was revenge.

The chapter on Hannibal had been the one that really caught his attention. Hannibal had used elephants in battle to terrify the ancient Romans. Wangle had never seen an elephant, but he had seen cats.

The one he was riding towards Chorleywood was a mature tomcat named Stripes by his previous owners. Stripes was frankly furious in the way that only cats can manage. Wangle had tied a harness on him, with steering reins and everything. Stripes had then gone completely berserk. It is very hard to train a cat to do *anything*. Only a will like Wangle's could have managed it and even then, he had picked up extraordinary scratches and lost a finger in the process. The other Dark Tollins treated Stripes with terrified respect whenever Wangle rode by.

RADIO

Even Wangle had given up on the idea of a *herd* of cats, like
Hannibal and his elephants, but it was no great loss. Stripes on
his own would terrify the Tollins of Chorleywood, Wangle was
absolutely certain. Stripes would terrify anyone.

After two weeks of living in hedgerows and eating
whatever they could find, Wangle's horde of invading Tollins
had reached the town of Henley and the banks of an enormous
river. Stripes could not be forced into the water and none of the
Dark Tollins liked the idea anyway. Over the years, a few Tollins
had been badly gummed by trout as they crossed rivers.
That wasn't a pleasant experience
by anyone's standards.

There was a bridge, but it seemed a bit exposed. Tollins are used to being invisible to humans, but no one could fail to notice a cat wearing a saddle with little stirrups.

From his high seat, Wangle looked down on the horde and saw they were fired up with enthusiasm. They always looked like that when he stared at them. It was safer that way. The way Stripes looked at them wasn't pleasant, either. It was a look that said, "One day, I won't be wearing a harness and I'll find you. When I do, you will regret it."

When Wangle turned back to watching the river, they all slumped, looking cold and miserable.

"We'll wait for night to use the bridge," Wangle said.

"Yes, sir," the horde replied in unison. There were thirty-two of them, which actually doesn't seem that many for a horde, but Tollins are not very numerous. For the Dorset tribe, it was quite a commitment. They'd rubbed soot on their faces. They even had a flag with a picture of a snake and the words

'Don't Tread on Me' as a motto. It was probably an adder, on the flag. No one minds treading on a grass snake. All *they* can do is look offended.

Wangle had persuaded the Dark Tollin Magnus to let him form a horde, but the volunteers weren't quite as keen as he was. No one could be, really. Wangle had not forgiven the Tollins of Chorleywood for his defeat. His hatred burned with a pure flame and he would not be turned back. It was strange, but only Stripes understood that sort of rage – all cats do. Wangle suspected the Tollin Magnus had only agreed to the invasion because he was too nice to say no to anything.

He leaned down and tapped his second-in-command on the shoulder.

"Kerton," he said. "Take two Tollins and scout the area. We'll make camp here until nightfall. Search the nearest hedgerows for something to eat. A mouse for Stripes, if you can catch one."

Kerton was a solid, mature Tollin, with ears that stuck out. He was used to following orders, though he raised his eyes at the thought of digging through hedgerows yet again. There was never anything good in a hedgerow. It wasn't like you'd come across a sandwich growing wild or something.

"Right, sir. Humble and Carter, you're with me." The three Tollins buzzed into the air, determined not to let Wangle down.

Wangle stared across the grey water. If he remembered it right, there were only around fifteen miles to go. On Stripes, he could do it much faster, but only by leaving the others behind. Even so, he thought they

could be on the outskirts of Chorleywood by the following evening. He'd show them the price of humiliating a Dark Tollin then. When he left the Chorleywood tunnels this time, he'd leave them in flames.

"In flames!" he said suddenly. The horde shrank back.

"Sir?" one of them ventured after a bit of elbowing from the others.

"Never mind. Get some sleep, lads. Busy day tomorrow."

Wangle dismounted at last, remembering not to let go of the reins until he had them firmly fastened to a tree branch. He also had to remember not to walk close to the teeth, or the claws. Stripes was *fast* and Wangle knew the cat watched him all the time. He doubted Hannibal had ever had this kind of trouble with an elephant.

CHAPTER FIVE

THE PROBLEM WITH A HAIR TRIGGER

"LOOK, GRUNION. I don't have time to muck about, all right? Yes, it's deadly. That is the whole point of a crossbow, really. If I wanted you to merely irritate a Dark Tollin, I'd get you to throw your foot at him."

Grunion looked hurt. He felt it was bad taste to mention his wooden foot. It was far too valuable to be used as a weapon anyway. There was literally only one of it.

He held the crossbow as if, well, as if it was as dangerous as it undoubtedly was. Ever since Dawlish had arrived, Sparkler had been even busier than usual. Grunion hadn't seen him eat or sleep for days. Sparkler was using the human library like a second home, looking for anything on warfare. He'd found

The Ladybird Book of Battles, but it was for children and Sparkler had gone on to serious books of tactics, sieges and all the tricks and history of field warfare. Almost in a spare moment, he'd knocked together the crossbow Grunion now held.

"I could *kill* someone, though," Grunion said desperately. Sparkler was already lost in a tangle of wires and battery parts. He had six transmitters working. It wasn't as many as he wanted, but Dawlish had no idea when the Dorset horde had set out behind him. They could be in Chorleywood at any moment and he still wasn't ready! He became aware that Grunion was still voicing his concerns.

"... and the end looks really sharp and Wing said it has a hair trigger, which I can't even find, and..."

"Look, Grunion. You won't have to shoot it, all right? If everything else works, they'll be so confused and frightened that they'll surrender. No one has to be hurt."

"So the crossbow is for...?"

"No plan of battle survives contact with the enemy, Grunion. Understand? You have to have back-up plans."

"So this...?"

"Yes, Grunion. What you are holding is a back-up plan."

Grunion looked at the object in his arms. It was made of iron and wood and it had a sort of vicious feel to it. He slotted an iron bolt into the groove and heaved on the stirrup to click the arms into place.

Sparkler froze with an armful of metal clips.

"Don't point that in here, Grunion," he said carefully. "If you want to practise, go outside."

Running footsteps made them both turn, though Sparkler did so while also taking two careful steps away from the crossbow.

"Message from the High Tollin, Colonel Sparkler," said the thin guard.

"*Colonel* Sparkler?" Grunion interrupted. "Promoted

again?" It had been Sparkler who'd discovered ranks, in fact. The High Tollin seemed to think that swift and regular promotion was the way to keep everyone working hard. If it went on, by the following morning they'd have an army of generals and no one to order about.

"As you were, Corporal Grunion," Sparkler replied, still keeping a wary eye on the crossbow. He turned to the guard, who had also begun watching it as Grunion waved it about.

"The message?" Sparkler prompted.

"Yes, sir. The scouts have spotted them, sir. The invaders, sir. They're coming."

There was a moment of breathless silence and then a sort of *boing* sound followed by quite a few other sounds, some of which involved breaking glass.

Sparkler heaved himself back to his feet, brushing dust off his trousers.

108

"I think we've all learned a valuable lesson, don't you, Grunion? Now take it outside and practise, please. How far away are the Dark Tollins... um... thin guard?"

"*Thin guard*, sir?" said the thin guard.

"I can't always remember your name; I'm sorry. Is this really the time to discuss it? No. How far away are they?"

"Less than a mile, sir. On the outskirts of Chorleywood. They'll be on the common by sunset." He paused. "It's Herbert, sir."

Sparkler looked around at the tangle of wires. He could finish one more transmitter, he thought. No, he was out of time and six would have to do. Everything else was in place, as ready as it could possibly be in such a short time.

"Get everyone into the Great Hall, ready for my orders. Right now. No time to waste... um..."

"*Herbert*, sir."

"Right, no time to waste, Herbert."

CHAPTER SIX

WHY HANNIBAL CHOSE ELEPHANTS

N STRIPES, WANGLE PADDED FORWARD as silently as he could. The rest of the Dark Tollins were flying just above the ground, keeping pace with him. The cat was at the point of a Tollin wedge formation that drifted slightly in the wind as it hummed towards the dim expanse of the common. The sun was setting and the rain clouds were still thick and black. Darkness was just moments away. On his right and left, two more wedges kept pace. He'd seen pictures of battles in the book and the armies always came in pointy wedges to the battlefield, like arrows.

The Chorleywood Tollins were not going to know what hit them. Wangle would then take great pleasure in explaining what had hit them and probably hit them again with the same thing.

His plan was simple enough. His three wings of eleven hardened commando Tollins would come in low and fast, heading for the three main entrances to the station tunnels. Before the High Tollin even knew what was going on, they'd have overwhelmed his guards and established Dark Military Law on Chorleywood. Or Military Dark Law, if you like. Either way, he had almost taken over before with just a few of his Dark colleagues. The sudden arrival of a proper horde would guarantee victory.

The first Wangle knew of the plan going horribly wrong was when the sky lit up. A firework soared into the sky and hung there, casting a red light over the common. Stripes made a yowling sound that chilled the blood. One of the horde said "Ooh", but Wangle silenced him with a glare and cuffed Stripes on the back of the head. Another firework flare followed and

112

then a third. He and his horde were exposed.

"Split up!" Wangle snapped. With a whir of wings, his commando Tollins shot off in three different directions. Wangle smiled. Even if the enemy knew he was coming, they couldn't catch them all in the open and he still had his secret weapon, claws and teeth and all. They'd shake off the Chorleywood lot with quick flying and then join up again at the station tunnels.

The last flare burned out and darkness came again, much darker and more frightening than before. Wangle was hard-pressed to hold Stripes back as they raced across the common. He heard the sound of marching feet in front of him and pulled on the reins to swerve away, taking his wedge in a different direction.

Voices! He heard voices over there as well and more marching feet! He began to panic as his wedge pulled a tight turn and set off once more. It was hard to know which way they were going in the darkness, but at least they were escaping the

defenders waiting for him.

For the third time, Wangle heard the tramp of marching Tollins. Somehow, Chorleywood had found itself an army. He pulled up in the air and the noise grew louder and louder until it seemed to come from all directions. Wangle slumped in despair. How had they done it?

"Put your weapons down and you will live!" came a voice. Wangle snarled and looked around. Sparkler. He knew that voice and he hated it more than any other voice in the world, even the Folk Singer who lived near him and couldn't hit A-sharp to save his life.

"There is still hope, lads," Wangle said. "One of the other groups will have got through, depend on it."

Out of the darkness, the voice came again.

"Do you mean those other two groups of eleven Tollins, dressed in black?"

Wangle blinked slowly. He hadn't intended to be part of

a conversation.

"Yes, I do mean them," he said at last, his voice a low growl.

"I thought so. They've surrendered. Sorry about that. Now please lay down your weapons and nobody needs to get hurt."

Wangle saw his horde sheepishly dropping their flint knives and cudgels to the ground before raising their hands in the air. It had happened so fast that he could hardly believe it. He watched in fury as Chorleywood Tollins ran in to collect the weapons, bearing them off in great piles.

Wangle kept his sword. He'd made it from one half of a pair of human nail-scissors and it was a fearsome weapon. He could still hear marching feet and he almost howled in frustration. There must have been Tollins all over the common, Tollins by the hundred, by the thousand even.

Slowly, he dismounted, walking forward with the cat's

reins in one hand and the sword in the other.

"How did you do it, Sparkler?" he demanded. "There aren't so many Tollins in the whole of the south of England. Did you hire foreign ones? Tell me that much. I have to know."

"You won't like it," said Sparkler's voice from the gloom. The sound of marching feet ceased with a click and Wangle had an image of a vast army stretching away in all directions. He saw his men being secured with chains and the flame in his heart blew white-hot.

Later, Sparkler was to regret what he did next. He knew he should have had Wangle quietly taken into custody. It would have been the end, right there. The High Tollin would have staged a lovely execution for him, with sandwiches laid on and everything. It would have been a family day out.

Yet Sparkler had worked hard on those transmitters and he was proud of them. In the tunnels under the station, the entire class of Tillets were still marching back and forth, back

and forth in big, heavy boots. The radio transmitter they had
with them had sent the sound to each of his radios in the field.
He'd created the sound of an army wherever the Dark Tollins
flew until they were so confused and frightened they practically
fell to their knees and begged to be allowed to surrender.
Sparkler should not have told Wangle any of that.
Unfortunately, that's exactly what he did.

With a wild howl, Wangle dropped the reins, raised his
fearsome sword and ran at the voice, his eyes terrible. There
were only a few Tollins standing with the radio that spoke with
Sparkler's voice. Sparkler was actually on the other
side of the common, having captured a different
group.

However, Grunion was there and he
panicked. The strange *boing* sound was heard

again and Wangle paused in his mad rush. He touched a hand to his arm and it came away with blood on it.

"Are you all right?" Grunion called in the silence that followed. "That's the second time that's happened. Honestly, I think someone could be hurt..." His voice trailed away as he realised someone *had* been.

Wangle advanced slowly, the crossbow bolt sticking out of his arm. All he could see was the Tollin in front of him. Somehow they'd beaten him again and someone was going to pay. He raised the sword above his head.

"You think you've *won*?" Wangle roared. "You haven't won. You've just declared war."

Grunion stared at him in slack-jawed amazement. No, not at him, *past* him.

Wangle froze, his eyes widening as he heard the pad of paws rushing towards him.

119

There are few more frightening sounds in the world.

Stripes had noticed the reins being dropped. He'd also noticed the way Wangle had turned his back on him at last. He'd waited a long time for just such a moment. With a triumphant yowl, Stripes leaped and snapped Wangle up.

In panic, Grunion tried to throw the crossbow at the cat, but Stripes was too fast. The cat spun in place and vanished into the darkness, carrying his yelling burden.

Sparkler listened, stunned, as Grunion told him what had

happened. Across the common, he sat back from his radio.
Wangle had been their enemy, but no one would have wished
for an end like that, even for an enemy.

The clicking of the handset brought him out of his trance.

"Yes? What is it?" he said.

"There's a Dark Tollin here called Kerton, sir. Wangle's
second-in-command," came a voice.

"Is that you, Herbert?"

"It is, sir, yes. Well done."

"What does this Kerton want?" Sparkler said wearily.

"He says he wants to make it perfectly clear that you have definitely not declared war, sir. In case you were wondering, sir. He says that this is a moment for our two Tollin nations to come together in a spirit of mutual friendship, sir. 'E's had a good look at the crossbow and the radios and he's very sure about it, sir."

Sparkler rose to his feet, his heart pounding with sudden excitement. With Wangle gone, perhaps they didn't have to repeat the mistakes of the past. Perhaps there was a future, after all. He laughed in relief as he reached for the transmit button.

"Tell him we accept his offer of peace, Herbert. Tell him there will be no punishments for his men. We'll throw a feast tonight and they're all invited."

He could hear Herbert grinning as he replied.

"Right you are, sir. He's also very keen to take one of

these 'amazing radios' back to Dorset with him, so
our leaders can talk to each other."

Sparkler hesitated.

"I'd agree with pleasure, but the radios only work
over a short distance. To reach Dorset, we'd have to get
an aerial hundreds of feet up into the air." An idea struck him
like a thunderbolt. "Hang on," he said, thinking. If he did it, he'd be
joining one part of the world to another. They'd never be alone
again. The sheer size of the idea swamped him for a moment.

"Herbert, we're going to need to get the wind-bag out of
storage," he said. "Tell him we can do it."

Winter had come by the time the great experiment was
arranged. Kerton and his commandos had returned to Dorset
long before, taking with them a working radio and an
enormous spool of wire as well as notes on making their own
wind-bag. They hadn't found Wangle, unfortunately, though

they did find a rather chewed saddle caught in a bush nearby.

On a misty dawn, with the sky a rare and perfect winter blue, the wind-bag rose above the common, carrying a thin wire with it until it was just a speck above their heads.

Sparkler tuned the radio, listening to voice after voice. The High Tollin was there for the momentous occasion. Wing had written a speech for him and it had a lot of flowery bits for the first contact between leaders. She waited with her father as well, watching Sparkler with a slight smile on her face.

More than once, Sparkler stopped in amazement as music came out, but he wasn't looking for music. It took time to find the thin and crackly Tollin voice. To human ears, it would have been the whine of a fly, or bad morse code, but Sparkler heard it in the midst of all the human rumblings, sweet and clear.

"If you can hear this, please respond," said the voice. "Chorleywood Tollins, this is an emergency. We need help and we need help urgently. If you can hear this please respond..."

RADIO

THE END OF
BOOK TWO

BOOK THREE

BONES

DARK TOLLIN TUNNELS

Vent

Dormitory

Entrance

Vent

Kitchen

Water Shoot

Bathroom

Jail

Snug

Jam Store

BERRY SHOOT

FOOD STORE

UP

LEFT

RIGHT

DOWN

THE GREAT HALL

CHAPTER ONE

THE WINTER OF 1924

THE HIGH TOLLIN WASN'T A FAST FLYER. In fact, no one could remember him ever leaving the ground. He certainly couldn't keep up with younger Tollins over any kind of distance.

When he'd insisted on going with them to Dorset, it was Grunion who suggested putting dragonflies in harness. He'd fussed and polished Blue Thunder until the insect was quivering. The High Tollin's own Yellow Peril completed the pair that would carry him over eighty miles. It had been simple enough to string a net between them, like a hammock, or a swing. A hammock is just a depressed swing, after all. Or if you prefer, a swing is just an excitable hammock.

It was a pale winter morning in Chorleywood when the team assembled by Darvell's Pond. It was that special hour when the grass is still frosted and there is silence everywhere. When the humans wake up, of course, it's noisy again as they clump about, but if the time *before* that had a name, perhaps it would be 'Tollin time'. Or dawn. If it had a name, that would also be a good one.

Sparkler and Wing were quiet, thinking through the journey and the dangers ahead of them. They didn't know what sort of emergency to expect, so they packed everything they could think of. The emergency kit formed a huge bundle that dangled below the High Tollin's hammock.

Grunion was towelling Blue Thunder like he was polishing a pair of shoes. Wolfenstein was watching the process with some interest and then turning his beady eyes on Sparkler as if thinking. Dragonflies have big eyes. When they slowly turn them towards you to make a point, you really know about it.

BONES

Sparkler took a duster from his back pocket and rubbed down the insect, who made a sort of *umph* sound. It has long been debated among humans as to whether dragonflies make any kind of sound. They do. It's *umph*, an expression of contentment.

"I still don't see why you need to bring Wolfenstein," said Grunion. Sparkler ignored him and it was Wing who replied.

"We do need a back-up flyer, Grunion. Just in case Blue Thunder or Yellow Peril run out of puff." Sparkler smiled at her, thankful for the support.

"Run out of puff?" Grunion said incredulously. "Run out of *puff*? Not my lad, I'll tell you that. I can't speak for the Yellow Pest over there, but ol' Blue won't let anyone down."

Wing found Grunion's confidence strangely irritating. Perhaps it was because she'd left her own dragonfly at home and she was missing him, or her, it was very hard to tell. Perhaps it was because Grunion wore his training jacket. It had

badges on it, with slogans like, 'In it to win it!' and 'Don't Fly By, Dragonfly!' Or perhaps it was a vague sense that the owners' club really should have let damselflies in as well. They were just like dragonflies, as far as she could tell. The one difference was that they could fold their wings. As a female Tollin, or a damsel, something irritated her about all the male Tollins refusing to let damselflies take part in the races.

With the High Tollin's two guards, Herbert and Daryl, the party was already up to six. Sparkler had the feeling that if they delayed any more, half the Chorleywood Tollins would be joining what was meant to be a fast rescue mission.

The cry for help from Dorset had come two days before, the very first message ever sent between colonies by radio. The problem was that it had stopped almost as soon as they heard it. They didn't know what the emergency was, or why the Dark Tollins of Dorset were in trouble. All they knew was that they had to get there fast. There had been no mistaking the fear and tension in that crackling voice on the airwaves.

Wing strapped her father into his hammock, tying him securely so he couldn't thumb to the two dragonflies and they took off, hovering above the ground with her father swinging gently between them.

"So far so good," she muttered.

"Ready, High Tollin, sah!" Daryl said, saluting. His friend Herbert looked impressed and added, "High Tollin, ready, sah!" The two guards smiled at each other proudly, while Wing rolled her eyes. In more ways than one, this was going to be a long trip.

"I feel I should make some sort of speech on this historic occasion," her father said from the depths of the string hammock.

"Make it as we go, please, sir," Sparkler said. "It's time to move."

The tiny group of six Tollins lifted into the breeze. If any humans had been there to see them, without blue glasses, all they would have seen was a pair of dragonflies flitting about on the banks of Darvell's Pond – carrying string bags.

"It was just two years ago that we met our Dorset cousins for the first time. I remember thinking then..." The High Tollin's voice faded with distance, thank goodness.

CHAPTER TWO

WOLFENSTEIN PROVES HIS WORTH

T TOOK FIVE DAYS JUST TO REACH THE SEA. All Sparkler and the others could do was get to the coast as fast as they could, but the dragonflies were labouring under the weight and Wolfenstein had taken his place in harness many times, allowing one of the others to rest. Sparkler was proud of him and gave him a bluebottle he'd caught during a rest stop.

The biggest problem they faced was that none of them actually knew where the Dark Tollins had their tunnels. The emergency radio broadcast hadn't given a location before it was cut off. The Dark Tollins they'd known had never mentioned their home except to say they were close to the sea. As the weary group struggled down to a sandy shore, Sparkler began

to realise Dorset had an awful lot of coast and an awful lot of
sea. He'd read about the sea in books. For once, that hadn't
prepared him for just how completely enormous it actually was.

He stood with Wing and Grunion, staring at the immense
blue watery thing. Somewhere beyond it, perhaps there were
Tollins who wore berets and strings of onions. They'd all heard
the legends. Perhaps in the past, Tollins had stowed away on
ships, or been trapped on one by accident. Sparkler could see
ships out there in the haze, like floating buildings. He felt his
curiosity twitch.

"One day, Wing. We'll cross the blue bit and see
what lies on the other side."

"Just the two of us?" Wing said, without
looking at him.

"And Grunion, obviously," Sparkler replied.
He thought for a moment. "Not your father,
though. He's a lovely, sweet old Tollin,

Wing, but he's not really a traveller, if you know what I mean."

Both of them turned to where the High Tollin was lying face down on a sandy clump of grass, groaning. One of the guards was stretching the High Tollin's legs for him.

"Let's get started then," Sparkler said. "We'll have to split up and search."

The one thing that might help was that Tollins didn't hide themselves. Before the whole blue-glasses problem they'd never had to. Outside the firework factory in Chorleywood, that still wasn't well known. Sparkler thought they had a chance of spotting the Dark Tollins in the open.

"I'll go with you and Wolfie," Wing said.

Sparkler nodded. "All right. Herbert, you go with Yellow Peril, down that way." He pointed to a distant cliff that reached out into the sea. "Grun, take Daryl and Blue Thunder. I think your father could do with a rest for a while, Wing. He can stay here while we look for Tollin sign."

If you are searching for deer, you look for deer sign. Sometimes that means deer droppings, but Tollins clean up after themselves when it comes to things like that. There are also deer prints, which Tollins don't leave because they are so light and spend so much time in the air. In short, tracking a Tollin is a real problem. However, they do leave a trace of dust when they touch the ground. That slight smudge was what they searched for, up and down the coast near a town named Lyme Regis.

It was Wolfenstein that found the first trace of dust. He was flying out ahead of them, enjoying the salt spray and abundant flies when they saw him bank and turn sharply, then hover over a spot on the rocks. There were no humans nearby to notice, not in winter.

Sparkler and Wing raced towards him.

"I trained him, you know," Sparkler said breathlessly. "It's like he understands every word I say. He even tries to roll over

143

when I give him the word."

"Don't you start," Wing replied. "I get enough of that from Grunion and his Dragoneers. Why not *Damseleers*, that's what I want to know!"

"Whose ears?" Sparkler said in confusion.

Wing gave him a look. It was quite a complicated look. In essence, it was a look that said, "You may be very bright, Sparkler, but not that long ago we kissed as Romeo and Juliet and while I realise that's a play and not real life, I honestly thought you'd have asked me out by now and you haven't." It really was a complicated look. It involved waggling the eyebrows quite a bit.

They reached Wolfenstein, still quivering over a smudge of golden dust on a stone.

Sparkler wasn't sure how he had annoyed Wing, but the sight of the dust put everything else out of his mind.

"That's it, all right," he said. "Tollins don't usually go far

from home. They have to be somewhere close by."
Slowly, he and Wing became aware that they were
at the foot of a huge cliff. They looked at each
other and then they looked up.

Above their heads, the cliff seemed to
stretch almost to the sky, a mass of black
stone about as heavy as Chorleywood. Far
up on the sheer rocks, Dark Tollins were
staring down at them.

"Oh," Sparkler said.

CHAPTER THREE

WHERE THE WILD THINGS ARE

TO SAY ENTERING THE DARK TOLLIN TUNNELS was a new experience would be something of an understatement. As far as any of the Chorleywood Tollins knew, no one from their colony had *ever* travelled this far from home. There were those ancient legends of Tollins who said "Bonjour!" a lot and enjoyed soft cheeses, but Sparkler half thought they were a myth. Cheese, as anyone in Chorleywood will tell you, should be firm.

The Chorleywood Tollins walked into the Dorset tunnels. The sun was setting outside and they left the light behind them, so that Sparkler wished he had brought a lamp.

"This is very... homely," the High Tollin said, trying to be cheerful. It wasn't. The Dark Tollins didn't go in for much in the way of comfort. The tunnels had been carved out of bare, grey rock and as they went deeper and deeper into the cliff, a heavy silence descended. All Sparkler and Wing could hear was their footsteps and slowly dripping water.

There were lights of a sort, once they were far from the outside. The Dark Tollins grew a rubbery sort of fungus that gave off a blue light in the tunnels. It hadn't been noticeable at first, but as Sparkler and the others went down and down, their eyes adjusted. In the dim glow, each of them could see how worried everyone else looked.

They'd had to leave the three dragonflies outside. Dragonflies are unable to fold their wings and the tunnels were just too narrow. It would have been childish for Wing to point out that damselflies would not have had that problem, but she did it anyway, with enormous satisfaction. Sparkler had looked back as he entered the tunnels and saw Wolfenstein peering in from outside. The dragonfly didn't look worried, because they don't have expressions. He looked just the same as always, but he *felt* worried, somehow. You had to know him well, that's all.

The Chorleywood Tollins knew they were nearing the Dark Tollin hall by its light. It appeared first as a golden glow somewhere up ahead as they trudged on and on with their silent companions. It was hard to know if they were being escorted as guests, or taken as prisoners, but with the return of light, they all felt their spirits rise.

The High Tollin had not enjoyed the journey into the cliff. He'd kept asking questions and no one had answered him. Even his own guards had felt oppressed by the trip and they were usually the ones who did all the oppressing, so they knew a bit about it.

One by one, they came out on to a ledge and shuffled along it to give those behind room. Before them was a vast orange and cream cave, hung with stalactites and stalagmites. Lamps swung from thin threads across the open space and stone steps led down to the distant floor. It did not look like something Tollins had made. The walls were rough and unpolished, bare of any decoration.

"What an extraordinary place," the High Tollin sniffed. He was a little bit put out that the Dorset Tollins had such an impressive Great Hall. He had assumed they'd be simple folk, living in rustic surroundings. Instead he was in a cathedral of orange stone.

"This must have taken them ages," Grunion said softly.

"Centuries," said a gravelly voice from behind him. They turned ever so quickly. A Dark Tollin had appeared out of the gloom. Like Wangle, he wore dark clothes and a small hat that seemed to be just the shape of his head, with a small brim, so people would say, "That's a hat," and not, for example, a skullcap, or teacosy. There was nothing cosy about this Dark Tollin.

"Centuries?" Grunion repeated nervously. "Those spikes are very nice."

"Stalactites and stalagmites," the Dark Tollin said in his deep voice.

"Gosh! So which of them are stal... actites and which are stal... agmites?"

The Dark Tollin opened his mouth to reply, then shut it again.

"I'm not sure," he said reluctantly. Off to one side, Wing shared a grin with Sparkler.

"Shall we go down then," she said to no one in particular. "After all, we *are* expected. You did send the radio message, asking for our *help*."

The Dark Tollin guard gave her a look. It was the sort of look you might see in someone allergic to nuts who has just discovered they are chewing a bit of peanut brittle. Like Wing's look to Sparkler

152

earlier, it was a complicated one and involved a lot of lip movement.

"There are *some* of us who wish that message had never been sent," the Dark guard muttered. "Some of us believe we should handle our own problems."

"Some of us, like the one standing talking at the moment, in fact?" Wing asked innocently.

The High Tollin had watched the exchange, his eyes switching from his daughter to the guard. That little battle could go on all day and he was tired. The High Tollin decided to take charge.

"Let's just go," he said. "Put me down on the floor, lads, somewhere close to a chair, or a chair-like outcropping of stone."

The High Tollin was lifted into the air by his guards, flown gently off the ledge and across the chamber. Sparkler, Wing and Grunion watched them go.

"After you then," Wing said to the grumpy Dark guard. He glowered at her before going back to his post in the tunnels.

"I hope the welcome gets a bit warmer than that," Sparkler said loudly. There were other Dark Tollins nearby. None of them looked away. They just stared, their eyes as cold as a Dorset winter.

"*Someone* must want us," Grunion said a little mournfully. "I mean, they did send the radio message. That Dawlish seemed all right. I wonder where he is?" The others nodded as they remembered the Dark Tollin who'd risked his life to warn them

of invasion that summer. It was true. Someone had to want them there.

"Come on, let's go and see," Sparkler said. The three of them buzzed up and spiralled down to the stone floor, far below. Grunion almost hit a stalactite, or it could have been the other kind, he had no idea.

CHAPTER FOUR

THE IMPORTANCE OF HOT TEA AND TOAST

BY THE TIME SPARKLER LANDED, Dark Tollins were coming out of the walls and lining up on either side of him, so that he found himself in a sort of corridor of Tollins, leading to, well, nothing, really, just an empty space on the stone floor. As Sparkler walked down the rows of silent figures, he saw a rather nice-looking sofa and armchairs being carried out of a side cave and placed carefully at the end of his path. He looked over the heads of the Dark Tollins and saw something similar was happening to his friends. Wherever they landed, they were being shepherded in the direction of the sofa.

As Sparkler came closer, he saw the High Tollin and his guards were already there. In fact, the High Tollin was sitting on

157

the most comfortable-looking chair.

Sparkler remained on his feet and so did Grunion and Wing. The guards took their usual positions behind the High Tollin, though they looked far more nervous than usual.

Without warning, the rows of Dark Tollins roared, a noise so great that Sparkler leaped back and the High Tollin clutched his chest in shock.

"Hail, Tollin Magnus!" they shouted as one. It was a very old-fashioned name for a High Tollin and Sparkler looked around for the one they meant.

"Steady on, lads, steady on," came a voice. Sparkler saw a Tollin about as wrinkled as the High Tollin. Sparkler looked behind him for the Tollin Magnus and then in astonishment, decided he was it. He was dressed in a slightly grubby robe and slippers and munching a piece of toast.

As Sparkler watched in surprise, the Dark Tollin Magnus wandered up to him and shook his hand.

"Good of you to come, dear boy. I hope it wasn't too much of a trial, getting here? No? Good, good. *Nasty* business. Sorry about the wind-bag. The string just broke, you see. Still, you got the message."

"Um…" Sparkler managed, but the Tollin Magnus was turning away. He'd spotted the High Tollin on the sofa and gone straight up to him.

"Budge up, old lad. That's the way."

It was not what Sparkler had expected. In fact, it was almost the opposite of what he had expected. He realised he had only really known Wangle. Perhaps not all Dark Tollins were quite as grim. He remembered the unpleasant one up on the ledge above the chamber, but in comparison, this Tollin Magnus seemed quite genial.

"Do gather round, room for everyone," the Tollin Magnus went on. "I do dislike having to raise my voice."

Wing, Sparkler and Grunion all took seats, not meeting each other's eyes. He had authority, the Tollin Magnus. It was the sort of authority grandparents sometimes have, which can be more powerful than shouting. It's not that you are afraid of them. You just don't want to *disappoint* them. The High Tollin was watching in open-mouthed fascination.

"Shall we do introductions?" the Tollin Magnus went on. "Is anyone peckish? I've only had a bit of toast and it's about that time." He made a gesture and a Dark Tollin officer marched forward in a clatter of heavy boots. He saluted sharply and then stood to attention, practically shaking with eagerness.

"At your command, Tollin Magnus!" he shouted.

"Good lad. Would you mind fetching me a few rounds of toast? Jam in a side pot? Anyone else? Shall I go the whole biscuit and order tea? What do you think? I'm so sorry, I haven't done names yet; how very rude. I am the leader of this merry little band, ahaha. Tollin Magnus is just a title, of course. Real name's Charles, but do call me Magnus, practically everyone does." The Dark officer looked absolutely crestfallen at this little speech.

The Tollin Magnus peered a little closer at Wing and blinked.

161

"My dear girl, I didn't see you at first. I have heard all about you, of course. Wing, is it?"

"Yes, sir," Wing said, smiling shyly.

"My son was very taken with you, I seem to remember."

Wing looked shaken.

"Do you mean Wangle, sir?"

"Ahh, poor Wangle. Such a terrible accident. I did warn him about that cat, you know. Still, least said, soonest mended, I always say. No, no, I meant young Dawlish, my dear," the Tollin Magnus went on: "He's talked of nothing else since he came back with that radio thingy. I'm surprised he's not here to greet you. So that's a pot of tea, toast for um... seven and perhaps two different kinds of jam. I think you'll find a little plum left in the pot near the pantry, captain."

"Right, sir. Tea and toast, sir! *Two* types of jam, sir!" The Dark officer looked ready to burst into tears, but he swivelled on his feet and marched away.

The rest of the introductions went quickly, despite a pause from the High Tollin, who didn't like to reveal his true name of Albert. He gave way in the end and the tea and toast arrived with military speed. For a time, there was no other sound except crunching and the squeak of a knife getting out a last dab of jam.

163

BOOK THREE

"It's such a pleasure to see our town cousins in the flesh, I can't tell you," the Tollin Magnus said at last. He sighed loudly. "I'm just sorry it's all too late."

"Too late?" Sparkler echoed. The old Tollin peered at him too.

"I'm afraid so. The charges have all been laid, you see. We're already beginning the evacuation. Come tomorrow morning, this entire cliff will be destroyed. All our homes with it. Most vexing. It's a crisis, you see. That's why I ordered the tea and toast."

"That's why you ordered...? I don't follow," said Sparkler.

"Oh, I always have tea and toast in a crisis. It doesn't affect the crisis, of course, but afterwards, well... you've had tea and toast."

CHAPTER FIVE

A TIME TO BREAK THE RULES

IGHT HAD FALLEN across the Dorset countryside. Magnus had agreed to an emergency meeting in his own home and Dawlish had shown up at last, red-faced and flustered from moving his family possessions to an old hollow oak in the fields. He had greeted Wing with obvious pleasure and Sparkler had taken an instant dislike to him, for reasons he could not completely explain. Wing seemed to be enjoying his company, oddly enough.

The meeting was going on late into the night. Around them, Dark Tollins were removing every last item from a thousand years of residence. They'd been at it for days and many of them were red-eyed with weariness.

"It all started with that human woman, Mary Anning," said Magnus. "I remember her, you know, though it must be seventy or eighty years ago. She started the whole craze for fossils, kept digging them out of the cliffs around here. Of course in those days, you could put a spade in anywhere and come up with some ammonites, at least. These cliffs are full of them. She was the one who found a plesiosaur, you know; first one anywhere." He saw the blank look on the face of his listeners. "Big fish thing, with teeth, made of rock."

"Is it still here?" Grunion asked nervously.

"Heavens no, it had been dead for a long time. A very long time, I think. I've certainly never seen a live one in the tunnels."

"Good to know," Grunion said.

"Now we have this new gentleman trying to do the same thing. At least Mary Anning did it with a little hammer and spade. That isn't quick enough for him of course. He's laid dynamite all along the ridge here. We watched the test explosions and we've seen the wires, leading to a plunger. Once that goes down, this entire cliff will slide into the sea and our hall with it." Charles Magnus sighed sadly and sipped his tea, though it had gone cold. "The tragic thing is that he's not even looking in the right place."

"What do you mean?" Sparkler asked.

"Well, you have to understand we've been in these cliffs for a very long time. Hundreds of years, maybe even longer. We know where all the bones are. I could show you places further along the coast with all sorts, full skeletons even – the strangest animals you'll ever see. Honestly, the whole coast is riddled with them, just not this cliff. That's what makes me a bit, well, irritable, you see. This human is going to destroy our home for nothing and then move on to another one. It's just so very *frustrating*."

"You could cut the wires," Grunion said. Sparkler shook his head.

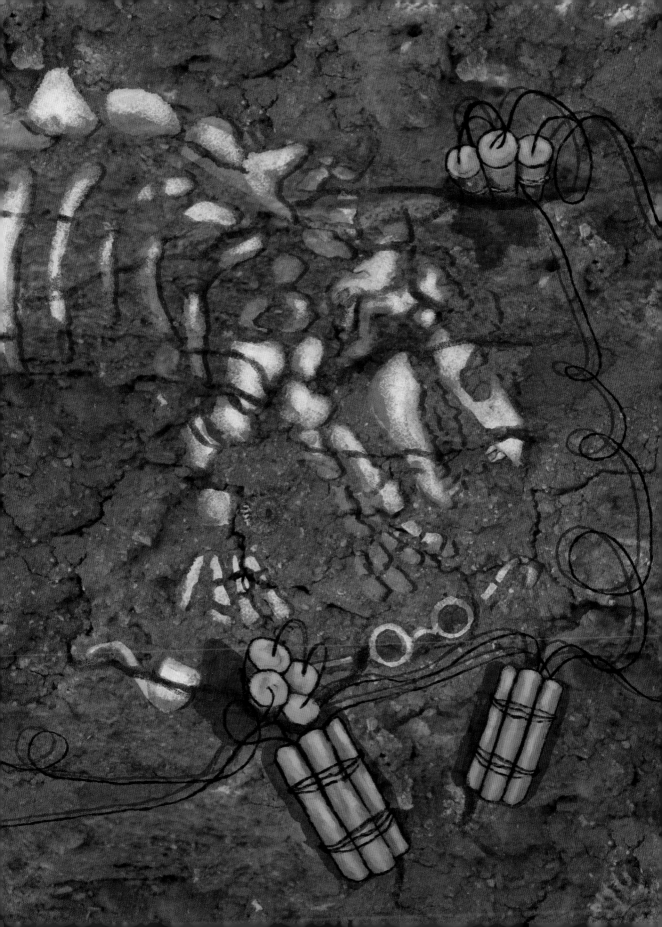

"They'd just bind them up again. You know what humans are like, Grun – determined. They don't stop easily, not once they have an idea."

"You stopped the bearded men, when you told them about making better fireworks."

Grunion had spoken innocently enough. There was quite a murmur of noise around them and he'd been warm and full of toast. As he finished speaking, he realised that the Dark Tollin's home had fallen silent. It was a shocking silence, so thick and serious that it seemed to spread out of the room and into the corridors and caverns beyond. Somewhere distant, someone dropped a plate.

Magnus leaned forward in his chair, clasping his hands together.

"Wangle *said* you broke the First Law. Of course, I didn't believe him. I have to say I thought he was making it up to blacken your name. He was one of a rather old-fashioned group,

you see. They call themselves the Sons of Dorset."

"I think we met one up on the ledge from the tunnels," Wing said.

"It's possible. I'm afraid they blame you for what happened to Wangle." Magnus looked at Sparkler and their eyes met for a moment. "Some of us understand a bit better than that. If you play with fire, or indeed cats, you have a good chance of being burned, or perhaps eaten. Wangle paid the

173

price of his ambitions." The Tollin Magnus shook his head sadly. "Perhaps I am too old for the challenges of a new century. For me, the Laws are all that keep us from chaos."

"Would that be a chaos worse than your ancient home sliding into the sea?" Wing asked. Magnus blinked at her.

"I'm not sure I understand, my dear," he said.

Wing looked at Sparkler. After a pause, he nodded and she smiled.

"You may not be able to speak to humans, Tollin Magnus, but *we can.*"

CHAPTER SIX

WAITING IN THE DARKNESS

IR ALFRED WEISS was not a man to insist on the luxuries of life. He'd hunted tigers in India in terrible heat. He'd climbed mountains in Nepal and suffered frostbite without complaint. He'd come late to the world of fossils, after seeing the entire skeleton of a mastodon* on show in New York. He'd been fascinated then and it wasn't long before he came home to Dorset and began exploring the part of it known as the Jurassic Coast.

It had taken time, money and energy to get permission to dynamite the cliffs. It helped that his cousin was the local mayor, of course. Alfred had gone to sleep that night with the intention of getting a good rest before dawn, when he'd pose

177

* Ancient elephant, bit like a woolly mammoth.

for a newspaper picture and then push home the plunger. He dreamed of dinosaurs as he slept, which became a little odd when a Tyrannosaurus Rex kept nibbling his ear. He waved it away a few times, but then at last, he woke up. He reached up to his face and found that he was wearing glasses. Surely he'd taken them off before he went to sleep?

It was dark in his little tent on the sandy hills by the beach. He'd chosen a spot where the wind wouldn't be too chilly, though he'd known a lot worse than a Dorset winter. He almost went back to sleep, but then he heard a rustling sound. In India, a rustling sound can mean a snake has decided to share your tent with you.

Sir Alfred sat up sharply and reached for a box of matches. No matter how brave you are, there is still something frightening about a tent in the middle of nowhere and the sense that you are no longer alone in it.

When he struck the match, Sir Alfred Weiss realised he

wasn't wearing his own glasses. Through blue glass, he found himself looking at a small group of winged creatures, sitting on his sleeping bag and watching him closely. With trembling hands, he lit a storm lantern and blew out the match before he burned his fingers. Should he call for help? His explosives team and labourers were all sleeping in the local pub. He was the only one who'd opted for a night out under canvas. The things watching him didn't look frightening, he had to admit.

"Good evening," he said after a while.

"It's already morning, I think," Sparkler replied, dragging his voice as deep and slow as possible. "Keep the glasses on – you need them to see us. Dawn isn't far off and we don't have much time, so listen closely."

In some ways, it felt like a dream. When he'd gone to sleep that night, Sir Alfred hadn't thought he'd be spending the wee hours in his striped pyjamas and a greatcoat, squeezing into cracks in the Dorset cliffs. Still, if they were telling the truth, it was worth a few risks. He'd never been a man to turn away from risk, even while tiger hunting, which was why he'd always been bitten on the front.

"Not much further," Sparkler called to the human. Dawlish was with him and the young Dark Tollin had impressed Sparkler with his courage, he had to admit. It was a lot to ask, to break the First Law. It had kept Tollins safe for a thousand years or more. However, some things are worth a risk and they had to have a guide who knew where the fossils were. Dawlish hadn't actually spoken to the man, it was true, but simply being there was enough.

The second challenge had been finding a way into the cliffs that was large enough to take a great clod-hopping human. They'd wasted a precious hour with maps before they'd found a place he could reach. Even then, it was going to be tight.

Sparkler watched in frustration as Sir Alfred Weiss wedged himself into the narrowing tunnel.

"Come on, it's almost dawn," Sparkler said.

"I'll have... to take my coat off," the man said, red in the face. He went back to get enough room and returned in just his pyjamas, with the storm lantern held in a trembling hand.

"Not far now," Dawlish whispered to Sparkler. The Dark Tollin was trembling himself, with tension and excitement.

They pushed on until the tunnel was so narrow that they worried the human would have to remove his pyjamas as well. No one wanted that, least of all the man himself. Great discoveries are almost never made by naked men, with the possible exception of Archimedes, who was in his bath at the time. All other great discoveries have been made by clothed

people. It's almost a rule.

Without warning, the tunnel widened into a cavern. Sparkler gasped as the storm lantern brought light to it for the first time in thousands of years. It made even the Dark Tollin hall look small. Water ran down across the far wall and perhaps that water had gouged out the cavern over the centuries. That was impressive enough, even without Grunion trying the echo and calling "Coo-eeee" until Sparkler nudged him.

The skeleton seemed to be made of black stone. It lay half in and half out of the wall and water ran over it, making it look alive. Who knew how long it had lain there, slowly being revealed by the torrent of years and water? It seemed to grin at them, but all skeletons do that. It's almost as if skeletons know some joke we haven't spotted yet. Perhaps they do.

"By the holy mackerel," Sir Alfred breathed as he came up and saw the cavern. His pyjamas were torn at the knees and he was out of breath, but he had never been so happy. He removed the blue glasses for a better look and then put them back on again.

"Will this do?" Sparkler asked him. Sir Alfred nodded, stunned. He didn't know what the fossil was yet. It looked a bit like a Rhomaleosaurus. He could see the huge fins and teeth. He shuddered at the thought of the seas it had known, a dark and ancient ocean.

"I'll remove the dynamite from your cliff, of course," he said. "I would have anyway, you know, once I knew you were there." He looked at the tiny creatures watching him so nervously in the lamplight. "Seeing you has been better than anything I could have dreamed of finding in these cliffs."

"The thing about fossils," Sparkler said seriously, "is that they don't mind being put in a cage, do you understand? If you tell anyone about us, that's what will happen to us. We trusted you with this." He hoped he'd made the right choice.

Sparkler relaxed when he saw Sir Alfred nod, then grin. For

a moment, he looked young again, almost boyish.

"Your secret is safe with me," he said.

There was no explosion as the sun came up. Now Sir Alfred knew where to look, there wasn't any need for one. While the newspaper reporter looked on in confusion, Sir Alfred led a party of his men down the beach until they came to a crack in the rocks. They thought he'd lost his mind when he vanished into it, but it wasn't long before they were all coming out again, their faces bright with excitement. Sparkler watched from high up on the Dark Tollin cliff. He was sitting on a ledge there with Wing, swinging their legs. He'd taken back the blue glasses he'd brought from home. He knew he'd taken a risk, but no one had been hurt and that made it the right choice.

"You know, Wing," he said, looking out to sea. She glanced at him and saw to her surprise that he was blushing. "I've been thinking."

THE DORSET DAILY TIMES

DINO-MITE!

"You're always thinking," she replied.

"Yes, but I've been thinking of other things this time," he said. "That Dawlish, for example. Do you like him?"

"A bit," she admitted. "He's a nice lad and he's the son of the Tollin Magnus, after all. It's a bit like *Romeo and Juliet*."

"Is it?" he asked.

"Well, two grand families, you know. The son of one and the daughter of the other..."

Sparkler scowled and she thought he might not go through with it.

"I did enjoy doing *Romeo and Juliet* with you," he said.

"Yes?"

"And I was wondering if you'd like to go out with me."

She put her hand in his and smiled.

"I'd like that very much," she said. Together, they sat and watched the sun rise over the sea.

BONES

THE END OF
BOOK THREE

THE END